Gnothi-Seauton

Knowing Oneself

by Mervis A. Brown

Ghonti Seauton is not a set of ideals or a philosophy floating in your head it is the knowing of one self and what matters in ones life and what matters is truth.

Dedicated to my son Tyrone who is the "Wind beneath my Wing."

Introduction

Even though *Cassi sought* to do everything right to prove that she had a handle on thing and she knew the processes and mechanics of this job. If one accessed this week they would think she just started. Even though it has only been 2 months she basically knew what was to be done. But this week it seemed like everything was done wrong. And even when she took the initiative and did what she thought was correct after discussion with the superiors it did not result in success. Her fear of the unknown had not bolstered any confidence where she was concerned. But Theodore was a bit more forgiving realizing this was just not her week.

Only thing Cassi learned is she must not only think about her task but that of the guy she worked for as he tends to overextend his budget. Resulting in shortfalls for which she had to prepare for. The action this week caused many of the problems she experienced over week however because Cassi was new to the concept of whole philosophy of thinking of herself and the fact she makes a less than 1% of what the man who is making the mega buck make. The crisis came upon her like a thief in the night and oh yes it almost destroyed her.

Well next week will be different she thought as she sat and looked through the window of the train she was heading home in. At this moment her mind also took on a reflective look at her life over the last year so many changes. The greatest being in a relationship that she thought was so beautiful became the cliché of a love songs was made of: she was only to find it is about a Love that Never Was.

Cassi went on a path of self revitalization and discovery, she sought to reinvent herself. In addition weight management i.e. losing some weight of which she knew attributed to the low self esteem she was feeling and the attitude to hide behind not being attractive of which only her own fears spoke of but no person to whom she had known ever stated. Cassi also decided to do what we girls say which is pamper ourselves and do the necessities of which we have now come to realize is essential to the prospect of looking good which is maintaining our hair and skin. The one aspect to which she had no problems in the reinvention of "me & me" many of the things like clothes she had always invested tremendous resources in buying the very best clothes that transcended times and fashion, clothes that were not fashion crazed but classic and timeless. Thus she now had the complete package for presentation, one could say the "Ferrari was now completely detailed". Another big step in the path to change was getting her divorce completed and being officially single of which she did immediately. Over the years she had fallen into a comfortable position with the separation that existed between her and her son's father they had their times of breakup and make-up. Through it all they maintain a level of friendship that whatever the circumstances they could confide in each other and to some extent they could look out for each other, of which they did on several occasion. However both knew when the day came when the legal bond was no longer in place all of that would ultimately change forever. They would still be civil and friendly however now there was no longer that intangible link or bond between them of husband or wife being joined as one. Now the only bond which is one that is linked forever is that of parents of a wonderful child.

Nonetheless the time had come to change that was the goal that must be accomplished as painful as that might be.

The journery begins...

"It is this belief in a power larger than me and other than me which allows me to venture into the unknown and even the unknowable."
Maya Angelou

DISCOVERING 'ME & ME"

It is the year Cassi was turning 40 and it has been her goal like that of her mentor Lady O to make this year the turning point in her life. She remembers the first time she heard the phase at the age of 40 women change dramatically. she thought this was just a cliché but when she listen to the story of O who at that age started down the road to be one of the richest women in her country, how after many failed relationships, bad judgment in career, dealing with self esteem issues, and then turning those negatives in to a positive force that propelled her to achieve more even at a loss of some personal goals such as children. She overcame

and then went on to inspire so many other women least of all

her. Unlike Lady O Cassi had achieved one of her utmost

goals and that was to have a child a miracle certainly

designed by God for her. But there are similar obstacles that

she also suffered from which she sought to overcome. Cassi

made a declaration that she would change how

She looked at her life and people in it and people who she

might come into contact with on this journey. One of the

new revelations she discovered was it is indeed a journey"

she agreed with that saying "as we sojourn this pilgrim's

pathway." As a deeply spiritual person she always reflected

on how and what the word of God says about us specifically,

and this passage of scripture stuck in her mind always" The

Lord orders our steps and directs or path." What that said to her was nothing she does is of mere coincidence or accident as it relates to God. He knew that with every decision she make and every action she took in relation to those decisions good and bad might result some positive or negative and she will deal with those consequences as she is guided. But the assurance is whatever the decision and how it may or may not affect her. Will she be able to endure? Because another great scripture now becomes evident in the grand scheme of things and that is "He will never see the righteous forsaken nor their seed begging bread." One thing she was sure of is as the seed of a righteous woman she aspired to be one her self always...So the long and short of it God is in full control of her life and he knows exactly what will happen and even though things might look like there is no solution there is always one because God is the one who has set the path and she am just sojourning through it..

Which brings us to year 2007 what a holistic year for Cassi she was turning 40; the year of change, in her eight year after the last committed relationship? The first thing she did was decided she need to get back to taking care of me not just being a single mother but a hot single mother...

When she was young girl she dreamt of having a home, a child or two and certainly the most handsome man as her husband. She secretly from the age of a teenager had dreams of this mystery man. She knew he was tall athletic and had the most caring smile one that reached his eyes he had the sincerest personality very easy going and laid back he was a man who although very smart and successful was so humble in his demeanor one would never guess he had the strong character of the great men of the times . Her perfect man was her soul mate the one who loved her for every flaw every flaw or imperfection, every good and every bad that he saw, experienced in her. He knew that just as she did that the love they will share would transcend time and space.

In entering every relationship past and present she sought this ideal in every prospective and current mate but as faith would have it none thus far had measured up. But as sure as night follows day and the sun and moon exist she was convinced in her spirit not her heart that he would find her or she him one day.

Discovering herself and knowing who she was, is crucial she knew in this journey to unite with this man. Belief in God was a foundation upon which she based her convictions and lifestyle. For many years she believed in an ideology with no scriptural facts a ritualistic type of worship that stifled her persona and her self expression. She walked the walk and talks the talk but in reality she never really accepted the lifestyle it represented. Rebellion was to the status quo was a norm for her amongst the brethren. Until one day she had a real renewal of mind, body and spirit and the very scriptures that was used to stifle and suppress her she used to release and liberate her. Cassi became a scholar of the word and sought out of driving force to know and fully experience and develop relationship which she never really had with

God. So much so did she embark on this pilgrimage that took her to higher heights and deeper depts., in the written word that she in turn became a teacher to others? The understanding to the word she knew was the foundation to any believer have a real relationship with God and knew that whatever way she was able to pass on her own experience and testimony to someone who could learn from it would make a tremendous difference in their life. Cassi changed not only her appearance she changed her attitude. She realized looking like a real woman not to garnish lust but admiration was not a sin, she knew that taking pride in your appearance and health is good for very one especially her. She also knew as a single mother for many years she would be attracted and opposite sex and they to her.

At age 40 she was ready to do what she had never done in her teens nor done in her twenties and that was meet men and develop relationship that will lead into something permanent and hopefully her soul mate will be there in that permanency..

~ Take a second out to think about this: in your life you search and search for the right person for you. Every time you break up with someone you get one step closer to that person. You should look at moving on as getting closer to meeting the one. ~

Ian Philpot

NEW HORIZON

Dating was a very scary prospect for Cassi as she never really dated much prior to being married...However one aspect of this new liberation that she was undergoing was to meet and interact with new people specifically men. The prospect of remaining single and living alone was no longer feasible for her. She desired companionship, she desired intimacy, and she desired friendship that came from a spouse. Cassi wanted a man; her own man who would love

9

her and care for her. For years she saw in the lives of friends who were married and who were single who dated the dynamics of their relationship and how they lived and grow. Some she envied some she pitted. But whatever their circumstances there existed a union between man and woman that she did not have and she desired.

Over this time of reinvention of "me & me" although Cassi still had a level of conservatism she had developed a degree of liberalism to many aspects of socialization. A friend had mentioned once while a gang of us girls was out celebrating a birthday that she intended to find a man by any means necessary at first hearing this she thought that her vagrant display of desperation was to be pitted however after further thought she realize she too would felt some level of desperation with the task of being "hitched". She went on to mentioned that she even have moved into the 20th century and have done internet dating, "umm" she thought about meeting total strangers telling you what they think you want to hear and knowing that they are people who can be very deceptive and dangerous. How could you know that what is told is true? But life is not be taken lightly it is a risk and a challenge and one must be ready or be left behind. She gave this prospect tremendous thought. Then one day she sat in her office and heard some co-workers mentioning the internet dates they had been on and how they were going to her surprise she realize that there are intelligent, decent and people who are seriously looking for love doing internet dating. The aspect was they lead busy lives that did not put them directly at a popular place to meet people and in addition they wanted compatibility and time to interact anonymously until can determine that a physical meeting must take place. With her busy life being a single mother she found it very hard to meet new people. She did not start, so taking the time to know someone through conversation and verbal and written communication was what she thought was the best thing for her to do.

Cassi started by going out more then, then she also decided to put her profile up on a few dating websites to see what the response could generate. She choose Christian website at first because belief was that the foundation of any good relationship must be anchored in similar faith and belief. And as her belief was in God the Father and the Son Jesus

Christ and the Holy Spirit she desired someone whom had the same belief. She did not put a photograph up at first because she was scared of it being used indiscriminately. However her guide in this process one of her best friends insisted and she quote" would you buy a ring without seeing it" she agreed with the logic and so she obliged and put one up. The hits she got were modest at best nothing to write home about she then added more information about herself, however nothing personal only work related and personal aspirations and instantly she got a ton of hits many were academically and career wise not in the same position as me so those were never considered then the other consideration was spirituality and financial finally which further narrowed the group tremendously. Her first response was from a

lawyer who resided in a separate country.

She communicated with that person for a while and even

went on a date. But when it came down to it level of

selfishness was displayed and she had to cut that link.

The online forum garnished many good prospects; however

this was not the most convenient way to establish

relationships so even though the communication was

interesting the distance posed a tremendous problem. She

realized she needed to have a game plan and that it must be

put into action in order for any feasible prospects were to be

had. She made a list of all the criteria's she desired in a

man, the must haves and maybe she will work with it

scenario. At the top of the list was spiritually next was

intelligence then was a sense of humor next was financial stability and lastly was looks.

Cassi anticipated that all the criteria's might not be as bountiful as one would hope for but at least the individual would have all of them. This enabled her do a very intricate weeding out of the prospects from all the sites she had enlisted in and "OH YES`` the pickings were very few after that. The good thing was the ones she had to pick from were the best of the best.

She made friends that even to this day; and eventually found the man who she believed would be her life long partner. One could say that after all that work she had found the perfect guy and experience a ``Love like no other `` but life is not a fairytale regardless of how we try and make it so.

This man was smart had one of the highest level of education, a moral compass so she thought, financial stability so it appeared and professed a belief in God he had stated. But illusions can seem like the real thing so easily especially if you truly believe in what is being shown.

In the beginning this man of hers was devote he called repeatedly every day and don't mentioned being online instant messaging or sending love notes via Blackberry or email. They had a constant link to each other. He expressed absolute concern in all areas of her life needing to know everything that happen. These qualities which reflected a "Worthy Man": protective, one who could be a provider, lover and friend? But lie can always be put to the test but truth stand alone and is blameless and clear. And what she came to realize is every action and even non action there was

a sinister motive behind it and although thereafter she would

realize the deceptiveness which was so blatant she could not

see while " being in Love " . But as they say love can be

blind, deaf and dumb, we see no evil hear no evil and speak

no evil. But evil is ever present in our midst so one never

lets their guard down, we must be wise and prudent in all

things. Be lead by your spirit your inner man that cries out to

you when the fear and doubt exist.

Now she believe she can hear the philosophers protesting that it can only be misery to live in folly, illusion, deception and ignorance, but it isn't -it's human.
Desiderius Erasmus

You, Me and Her

Cassi love of reading .taken her to various paths of consciousness and reasoning. The motto "Knowledge is key and knowing is half the fun" had been her creed for as long as she can remember. She had endeavored to know how people react, think and do things and the only place that has been her source of information has been in books. She believe in a different life, she would have launched into writing books about love, hate, good bad and the indifferent...

On her path of self discovery she has tried to redefine her perceptions of how relationships should be and how she should go about having them. In her current circumstances one of the most tiring times was going through this dark phase. At a time when all should have been happy and joyful in a relationship a first stage of betrayal started. A phenomenon which can only be coined emotional infidelity was being inflicted upon Cassi. Loosely defined as a time a person whether with a pal, colleague or former sweetheart-becomes as important or in her case more important than the partner. To many it is not recognized as a full fledged affair however an emotional affair. These relationships start innocently, but it is a slippery slope where boundaries which should have been set have been abandoned. By the time people realize they are in deep and the damage is done. In Cassi case because she had experienced infidelity before she immediately recognized the signs and steeled her heart from the devastation she knew was sure to come.

None-the-less like the words of a song that echoes her every sentiment at times it felt like the world was closing in on her, it seemed like her dreams would never come to be. It put her deeper and deeper into herself of fear. Inasmuch as she remembered those faithful words "there is nothing to fear than fear itself". Her trust was broken and the fear was there will she ever be whole again.

For argument sake we will call the heartbreaker Jeff and the woman Silvia. .

Silvia was a single woman with a child who found the time to be involved in a committee that Jeff overseas she had the unique position as secretary but according to Jeff she was his personal assistant. Now as person who have been around men and working with them at all levels Cassi was well aware of the temptations the close bonds that can be at such times. However boundaries must be maintain to be professional and the intimate and personal with the spouse or life partner and the social friendship must be non-committal and impersonal. Unfortunately, these two individual was never taught that lesson and blatantly went about there relationship in the most disrespectful manner to cause Cassi as much hurt and pain as they saw fit. What made matters worst was the relationship with Jeff and her was in the early stages (they had just united in marriage) and was undergoing tremendous testing the least of which was this issue. But instead of putting his energies and time into building and ensuring the intimacy is true in the relationship he committed himself to with Cassi her husband went about ambivalent about their mutual happiness. At the start of this betrayal the initial response was to hurt back as well in like manner. However she knew that, no good would result by such an action. The mere fact of know how much pain she was experiencing meant that doing the same would only make her feel worst because it might hurt him but her self respect would be lost and she would be no better than he was. As a friend had mentioned she was going through fire and all that it would do is burn off the impurities and leave fine gold.

Because of the vow she made Cassi hope that God would

shine a bit of light into the heart of her husband, even though

she was now sure had no feeling for her. But as they say

hope springs eternal and unfortunately no care can come

when there "is no love ".

There is no principle worth the name if it is not wholly good.
Mohandas Gandhi

Wicked One

Being declared wicked is in and of it self a very sad commentary. Nonetheless to be declared in the midst of a relatively calm argument by your husband can only is described as if one was sentenced to be hanged by the toe nail. At least for her that what it was, she was declared by many has having a very pure calm and peaceful nature, in fact she so avoids conflict that when anger does surface in her person it is regarded as passive aggressiveness even by her very husband who now reason that she was wicked. To her the hurt and pain was never required in any resolve living by the cliché "what goes around come around", she never

once believed in the creed an eye for an eye. Furthermore as

a Christian by nature forgiveness and love she earnestly

made her convictions upon which stood.

So why her husband called her wicked one would never

really know unless he released the intent of his thoughts,

mind and heart at the time the statement was said. However

the scenario was as such. A period of calm existed for the

couple and things were civil. Basic communication existed,

although her husband still made him self less friendly and even

more distant, however she believed that as he declared the work

commitments were occupying his thought, his time, his emotional

responses his very being there was little time and interest for

anything else especially her. Cassi knew his love was almost

gone since he declared it so. But sold out to her convictions and the vows she made she would never leave she would be there under whatever circumstances even to the bitter end. One night just after having a thoughtful evening and venturing off to bed, as she approached her bedroom door she heard her husband on the phone, she entered and proceeded to her closet which was just on the other end of the door. Even though the closet was a walk-in closet and she barely closed the door in order to get undress and put on her night clothes she could hear even from across the room the person on the other end of the phone and just like on other occasions it was a woman who appeared to rambling about how she felt her husband in response began to declare how earlier in the day when he saw her face was swollen ect. , at that point she open the door and then she heard him finalizing the call declaring he would connect with her tomorrow. This was upsetting to her has there has been other occasion when her husband at wee hours of night get on the phone with female individuals and have very endearing or engaging conversations while at the time he not merely say two words to her his wife. That same evening he barely talked to her while she sought to select information about his day what was happening in his business all he did was dosed. In truth she should have let this too pass however she could not sleep beside him she need to let him know that his constant attention being given to these females whomever they are to the neglect of this wife was killing her and she detested it. Well she battled and finally got the courage to tell him by waking him up to do so. At that time he did not discuss it but declared he would talk about it the next day.

Next morning as they both stood at the breakfast nook her

husband declared that he was absolutely upset at the fact she

woke him up and furthermore what was wrong with him

having a conversation with his friend they intend to intact

business. His tone which was none too pleasant surprise, so

although he asked for her to respond she refused to avoid a

confrontation especially since this was a bad time she head

to work in 2 minutes not to mention she just did not want to

get into an argument.

Later that evening her husband met her in their bedroom and

in a very stern and frustrated voice requests her to correct a

situation she had worked on for him. Again she understood

that this better be done or else. So next day she made it her

business to resolve the issue and just to ensure that her

husband knew the extent of her efforts to do it she emailed

him and text him however the text coming from her

computer ended being multiple text. So later that evening to

discover or rather disclose this her husband first lectured

about a can he found in the garbage which she believed her

son may have put there instead of the recycle bin, but to her

husband it was very wrong and most certainly although she

noted she would again go over the difference in the recycle

bins with her 10 year old son her husband mad the problem

her problem. Then the stage was set he then launched into

the text messaging.   Then conversation was not yet finished

as he dismissed any response from her he beckoned her to

the bedroom where after closing the doors so that the boys

would not hear he again launched into the issue of text

messaging, then she made a point after he declared he found it difficult to talk to her because she choose to speak when she want she made not to him he did the very same and more he would dismiss any comment she had and promptly walk out on it. From the look on his face she knew she had just hit a sore spot. And he was pissed that she could make such a statement. He declared when did he not allow her to talk and mentioned that morning he asked for a response but she refused to talk she told him she did not because she could clearly see he was angry by the raised tone of voice and attitude and then he said she had ample opportunity to talk she no she did not but before the words or explanation could be finished he looked at her and called her wicked she was VERY WICKED he declared. Be gone on to further talk she was dumbstruck she just looked at him. Then he declared do you have anything to had she just stated just to be clear of what she was being label. So he said she was wicked and looked him in the face and he stared back and said yes WICKED.

Cassi was devastated she jumped in her car sped off and just to get air. Almost ran into two cars. But God was watching over her she came back home shortly after and cried like a babe. To she that was the worst thing he could ever say to her. The word hurt took on a different meaning that night for her. Her like flashed before her eyes and she just saw after all that she had done given been to this man, who was her husband, lover and one who promised God he would protect and take care of her he now declared her

WICKED. She was broken her heart felt like it was just ripped to sheds.

Next morning Cassi looked down at the rings she wore which symbolized the unity that should have existed between them and she took it off making a vow never to wear them again until he apologized and gave them to him. Funny he gladly accepted them. He had absolutely no remorse, she hurt even more because his no apology meant it was not a mistake he meant every word. To add insult to injury he sent a text note to declare that there is slight difference between wicked and dangerous. She saw this and smiled, so she should be thankful he did not also call me dangerous, because then she would certainly be a threat to humanity. She realized the marriage was now definitely although she tried to revive it in name only and be preparing one day as soon as her income is no longer need she will be served divorce papers but unfortunately this time around she knew ahead of time so she will be preparing for the eventful day. What does wicked mean, she looked it up and it was explained like this she excerpt.

Wickedness is a synonym for "evil" and therefore stands as the very antithesis of Christianity (i.e. opposite to and against Christianity)! How is it that a Christian can use a word that means everything God hates to describe something that God has intended to be good? Indeed, in Matthew 12:24-32 the Pharisees did something similar by attributing the work of the Spirit to demonic activity. Jesus called this blasphemy and went on to state that such a thing was unforgivable!!!

Therefore, it appears that what is really "wicked" is the

misuse of the word "wicked"!

Misusing words causes their meaning to be obscured and this has far
reaching consequences. The blurred meaning of "wicked" also blurs the
distinction between good and evil, and right and wrong. If we are not
careful, the next generation will descend further into relativism, because
they have little concept of the difference between right and wrong. In
addition, the word "wicked" is used in the Bible over 450 times -- and never
in a positive sense. When people read about the "wicked men of Gibeon" in
Judges 19:22, we do not want them to think that these mean were "really
cool." On the contrary, these men raped, murdered and butchered a
woman! Such people are completely the opposite of what God wants us to
be like.

The misuse of "wicked" has largely come about due to the popular media.
Again, this is the spirit of the age telling people in a subtle way that there are
no real absolutes -- no such thing as right or wrong. But in Romans 12:2 the
Apostle Paul writes: "Do not conform any longer to the pattern of this
world, but be transformed by the renewing of your mind." Note that this is
not just a warning or a piece of advice, but a COMMAND. We are
commanded NOT to be conformed to the pattern of this world, which
includes the misuse of the word "wicked." We are commanded to renew
our minds, and start using language properly so that communication
remains meaningful and the message of the good news of Jesus Christ
remains clear and simple

So now Cassi must decide what and how she will survive

this relationship. The first thing she did was let her husband know that she knew what his statement meant. Next she informed him although the hurt will never be forgotten she forgave him she had to as a Child of God. It's not about him it's about her soul salvation and the unbelievable thing she did further was apologized to him. Because whatever led him to a point to use that word must be hurt so she wanted him to know she intended no harm or hurt to him. Now it was left up to him to react or not to... she believed he would do nothing because his intent using the word was to hurt her and he accomplished that so why alleviate any pain in fact she believed he would further alienated her and treat her with even greater disdain. But now she was free her soul liberated she knew God will take care of her and bring her out with a testimony so she just carried on and did what he

knew she should as a wife.

The story of life is quicker then the blink of an eye, the story of love is hello, goodbye

Jimmy Hendrix

GONE FROM ME I NEED YOU NO MORE

For the past week or so Cassi was told by the husband that she would be getting a very detail response to the some questions she asked of him. As she waited with anxiety and fear she knew the mere fact that taken over a week for him to respond means the response will not be good. Anyway all she knew nothing is left to fear than fear itself. The morning was bright and fair... This would be a great day she started her first Karate Class. She hope she don't embarrass her self in front of all those kids. But she could not resist the look of joy on her sons face when he knew she was doing classes with him.

As she sat at the breakfast nook around the corner came her husband with a broad smile on his face saying. Here is the letter you have waiting so long for. She took the letter looked at the outside in one of the nicest handwriting she had ever seen it was nicely addressed in her legal named. She timidly opened it and noticed immediately it was dated and contained 4 pages all nicely typed. As she started to read the letter there was immediate apology and then blames of her actions ...Oh! Oh! this was not going to end great she thought, further on there was self praise from him stating how and what he has done and what she did not do. She skimmed over the rest and went to the final paragraph it stated clearly "In light of this we should separate" then further went on to detail how a separation would be enacted. At that point she closed the letter went to find him, of course he was in the office where he normally stays... She beckoned can she approach and he signaled yes, she then stated , she read his letter and just so she was clear you request a separation. He stated in an affirmative 'YES'. He did go on the reinstate what he wrote in the letter and she simply stated to him from her point of view he wanted things his way or no way at all. She spoke to the fact before taking such drastic steps on a very fragile relationship why don't they just get-together and do counseling and again he state 'NO' he wanted a separation in place first.

At this point even being fully composed reality hit Cassi like a bolt of lightening and she realized she was cheated, lied to and pretty much taken grave advantage of. The Prophetic statement he made 3 weeks before their wedding materialized in an instant... She now was made into a fool by this person whom she pledged her life and love to. She knew after her second appeal for reconsideration at that moment of the second ' NO' the marriage was over and this person not only hated her he despised her greatly because the callous and unremorseful way he went about destroying, her well being and life it was so meticulously done. She looked at him then and saw a stranger, it went surreal to her. It was as if she saw him for the first time and every evil thought he so carefully hid now shone like a beckon from his eyes and face. She realized she must regroup and realize she is seriously at war, a war for her well being and that of her child a war to destroy her peace of mind an emotional war and lastly a physiological war.

The pain seemed overwhelming and almost too much to bear because even though she realized there was no going back to the what could have or should have been this spelled the end of a marriage. This was a brief one but the end of something that should last forever. Death brings grief and pain and at this time she was feeling enough of both that made her know she could not cope on her own. But she would do all she could and more because she not only had herself to take care of she had her son to look after as well and above everything and everyone HE was the most important part of her life.

Peace is not merely a distant goal that we seek, but a means by which we arrive at that goal.
Martin Luther King, Jr.

COUNSELING

Counseling was something that Cassi felt was only for emotional wrecks people who were weak and who did not have a good relationship with the Lord. God was her counselor he was the one who ordered her steps and directs her path. Cassi had built her relationship with the Lord by studying his words and prayer. Whenever life challenges had her down she took refuge in her faith. She would seek the Lord answer through prayer and fasting. Even going through the turmoil of the relationship she knew her sanity was held because her believe held her in tack by the God his divine grace and mercy.

However the overwhelming emotional stress was something she definitely need to have a second ear with, although she hated that her husband had mentioned seeing a counselor on one of his more pathological and manipulative dissecting of her character and life she realized counselors would give an honest second opinion for the issues that troubled her mind.

In seeking such a tentative hear she again knew someone who was grounded in the word of God was best suited to help someone like her who is lived by the word. She went to the church she attended and sought the services of the Pastoral counseling.

When Cassi entered counseling the intention was to see where she had gone wrong by her actions to cause her broken marriage. Cassi struggled to deal with the realization

and subsequent marriage was ending. In fact within Cassi

work in counseling reinforced her beliefs and it enabled

Cassi to know that the self blame for failure in her past

relationship especially her ill faith marriage was not entirely

hers. She found a peace in the fact that even this too will

pass.

Being deeply loved by someone gives you strength, while loving someone deeply gives you courage.

Lao Tzu

Love Letter to the Love That Never Was

When one does self analysis you should reflect both on

the good and bad. Cassi thought was there any good?

She could say yes many times when all was well in the

world and in the world that existed between her and her

husband when the Love she thought existed felt

overwhelming, she felt safe, secure and loved. But now

it was like looking into a looking glass only dimly

because you never know real and true love until it is

tested, when you are face to face with choices and our

response to those choices reflect what and how much our

actions and statement can build or destroy what we believe we have. She remembered a sermon which she heard about words and the tongue and how it can bring edification even life and how the same tongue and destroy and ultimately kill.

Cassi realized in reflection the truth always is before us about our current circumstances and now we must respond to the truths. She had been counseled in the temporal and in the spiritual. But as usual the essence of who we are lies in the spiritual so without a doubt that counsel has brought to her personal truths.

'The first thing she did was to accept that blaming herself for the failures she been confronted with does not help just as un-forgiveness' will not heal her broken heart.

So from the beginning when did this decline started, she asked herself? Was she too naive or was she fooled into believing that she had found someone who unconditionally loved her. The evidence is clear naivety...Or was it a deception that matured over time. Even in that content it rings true because she remembered a line from a song which stated" True Love asks for nothing it accepts us the way we are it strives to care when it is becoming hard to care."

The day or night of recognition came when her husband said to her one night after they just finished having sex, "Not love Making" but sex that he only loved her a little bit. She realized their was a measurement to the amount of love this man had to give her the same one who just 3 month earlier he had "vowed before God and a bunch of Black people that he would love, honor and protect her for better or worse, richer or poorer, in sickness and health until death they will part". The Words which in the lives of many people have become an idle joke they should just cut that out and just say "Hey baby he said ' she will be here only if you don't piss me off or until she find a white woman or she cant get it up anymore'. Because she could certainly believe that statement more than this traditional "mumbo jumbo" that really even for so called Christian men like her husband meant "Jack Swat".

She searched to find transcript of emails from the "luvie –duvie" days of courtship, and the sentimental crazy lyrics she had believed. She had kept everyone, so one can realize how hard it was for her to give to her husband the wedding rings he gave her but a stand had to be taken and that was just tough love some women flush rings down the drain other sell them she wanted him to have then he can do what ever he wanted even give then back if he was a good man and hope she would forgive and take them and that be a new starting point in there lives together, but to the contrary that was never his intent , pride and prejudice took president in his life. She read a couple emails but found one that really showed her how naively she feel in love with the concept off what true

love would be and inadvertently with the wrong man.

He wrote "Babes, she listened intently to the first song you sent me. As she listened she smiled and gasped knowing and hoping that these words proved true and lasting for us. She did like her wake up call very much. She could do that every day for the rest of her life. She wants to love you and be into you like you desired and expressed. She is willing to work on it with all she got. When are you moving in.......?"

....

Quote"she really does miss you for real...weird as it might be.... You brought some thing in her life. The reason she asked you to call is that she miss you terribly. Now that you are in her life, she doesn't want to be alone. She have been longing and feeling you since we met. And although she submerges herself in work as an antidote, the pull and tug on her heart from you overpowers her lone ranger tendencies. She have come a long way, though sometimes she wonders about herself... she attributes it to your innocent and pure love. She is planning the marriage before the wedding and will keep you posted. Again she asks when you are moving in.

Those emails declaring the goals aspirations and dreams that of a life that would be filled with love not one filled with criticism "oh no " Correction feedback as according to her husband and then ultimately his analysis of her character that she was the wicked, lacking credibility, integrity and honesty of course in light of his superb character; one that refuse to acknowledge any fault to breaking her heart and flushing the marriage she wanted to maintained down the drain with a letter stating we must separate and go our separate ways after 5 months of marriage, an ego which ridicule and question her integrity for not disclosing that she only became finally divorced after 8 years of separation 7 months to the date they were married although the process started 2 years prior to meeting him, nonetheless he held the resentment and went though to with the marriage only to use is a point of characterization, one in light of his self centeredness and ego . She realized even now she loved him "STILL" and even through the months of dysfunction, hurt and doubt she always will. You see he was the not the first man for Cassi but he was the first man and only man she really feel in love with her Love was tested and tried and without doubt she thought she loved him "STILL . An exercise in futility but it the exercise she choose to take, it was a love she carried that was unconditional. As the life she hoped for hanged in the balance she can only see to be true to person who she was. She struggled with feelings of resentment after every argument but now she was at peace, even knowing he had no love for her that was just the cross that she must bear. Emotional humps are a part of life. She remembered the words of one of her favorite songs by Stevie Wonder" Always" the words she will love you forever. And just has kindness knows no Shame. True love asks for nothing, Life has given love a guarantee to last forever and day. It was recalling the words of this song that Cassi realized her lost LOVES were just not TRUE. Every one she loved asked in some cases demanded something of her for their own selfish pleasure. Life does not guarantee you will find TRUE

LOVE but it does provide the opportunities for you to locate it one day.

Again to her foundation to endure and carry on for as God so loved sinful men he gave his only son to die for them and yet they continue to disregard Gods Gift and love for them. She does to her husband and extends her love because someone did for her even though she was not worthy and that is God. But there comes a time when even when you stand do all you need to do you must stand and be you.

Do not dwell in the past; do not dream of the future, concentrate the mind on the present moment.

Buddha

WANNA KNOW WHY...

Cassi once read a book entitled "How Did she Get Here" by Barbara De Angelis and like many of the books she read through her time of turmoil and self analysis this book had a life changing effect. Not only was the author early life similar in some regards to mine it spoke of overcoming in face of adversity and disappointment that she found effective in her goal to move ahead...

The author was married twice and had children and career and a life of which lead one day to the asking how she got here. She asked herself especially since the end of her very brief second marriage that question. She sometimes wonder if she will every really get over that chapter in her life. It is definitely a struggle and a challenge to be cool with it... But when you totally put your confidence and trust or you your life and others to another and they end up hurting you so dramatically and lead you losing all trust and faith not only in them but there species(males) it is definitely tough..

Cassi once asked the question of her former husband as to why did you marry me if after 5 months you would want separation, why did you profess love to me when clearly you did not love me, why did you make me sell her home and move; uprooting her life and child saying you would protect and provide for us then you turn us out of the home we now come to share with you? Why? Why? She asked why to all these and may more questions. But in reality what, she should have asked is why you are such a self serving, egotistical, cold hearted bastard. WHY! WHY! Walking with the sword of the spirit (The Bible in one hand) and then the sword of evil and hate in the other hand but instead using the bible to up lift you used the evil sword to kill emotions and destroy hopes and relinquish goal of joy... she Want to Know Why?

When she read the book a 'Purpose Driven Life' it was at a point when she felt that she was on the threshold to untold miracles in her life... |She believed that because she was like Barbara De Angele's in her book going through uncertainty and unlike her financial hardship

and like her emotional turmoil over her relationship, job.

A breakthrough was about to occur, you know the saying

it never rains it pours, well it was pouring on her. But

looking at her you thought she had it all together. But

inside she was torn up... But as normal she never let her

guard down she must always be strong and after having a

child that only reinforced her resolve to be a superwoman

in every way... The Book Purpose Driven Life gave her

back vulnerability; it gave her assurance that whatever

life purpose is it will always be found in God. She knew

this for sure. Now here she was back where she once

was reliving the questions that leave asking WHY...

thank God she never desired to ask God Why. She knew

even in the midst of all of what she was going through

the Purpose is being revealed. Cassi had lived and

believed and still do to this day... All things work for

Good to them that love the Lord and are called by his

purpose...

Turn your wounds into wisdom.
Oprah Winfrey

STAND GIRL

As Cassi continue to determine where and what she will now do to pick up the pieces of her life. She knew that one thing was absolute she now stood alone. And whatever course she must take to put back the pieces of her shattered life it must be with determination and confidence and above all put her trust in God. It was only God who would take her through this uncharted water, the terrain looked rough and certainly there would be hills and valleys high and low. Some how, she had an inward assurance that all will be OK.

It was remarkable how thing started to unfold in her life one dream shattered but another is emerging. The hand of the Lord was evident in all the things that unfolded. While being confronted with new challenges such as not only being told that the marriage was at an end was told to vacate the home she resided in. This was to her as again another blow to the gut, just to think how months earlier she had her own home where she and her child lived in relatively joy and peace. And now she was almost homeless, it took great strength push what if aside and focuses on moving forward.

Cassi felt a new awareness of herself, some thing burned in her being not hate but a determination to really close this chapter of her life very fast and totally. She felt she still loved her husband but undoubtedly in an absolute different way than when she wed him know the 'Eros' love no longer radiated within her being. She no longer saw him as the life-partner, she now saw him as a person she meet while on her pilgrim journey one of the many who God had place within her life for a purpose and even though one may say what purpose can a man who hurt her so irrevocably be he served his purpose that she certainly believed.

She fought for her job and maintained it she sought a place to call a new home and found it and now she decided as the year came to close here and now she will make her pledge that her life is to be utilized by the Lord her STAND in the words of God. "He will never see the righteous forsaken now their seed begging bread". God has been her source and her comforter at all times, he made provisions and ways for her that she never thought would ever be. Well even going through this catharsis, Cassi's husband went on a relentless course of actions to get her to move out of the house. He accused her and totally ostracized her son he even stooped as low as to accuse her of tampering with his files and personal property by giving her a hand written note called "Theft and Security". She had reached the breaking point she realized for the safety of her and her son she not separate by moving out the house as soon as possible. To Cassi it appeared that her husband now was totally emotionally as he used the term" Out to Lunch". He saw nothing but what ever appealed to him and made him feels happy.

The self centeredness and ego was limitless. She

proceeded to make the final arrangements to move and of

course move on with her like as he once wrote, "separate

completely and move on in life and love ultimately".

She realized even though this was going to be the most

tiring times in her life it would be the most defining time

as well. She packed up all the belongings she had and

had acquired and she took her child and moved as was

requested.

*In three words she can sum up everything she learned about life: it goes on-*Robert Frost

A New Day A New Start

Oh what a difference a day makes! Oh what and a

difference a change makes....

She woke up to the sound of silence to the feel of

oneness to the smell of the perfume "Pleasures" on her

pillows. She opened her eyes and the surroundings

looked unfamiliar but looked serene some thing out of a

novel. "Clean clear walls light clear beautifully draped

curtains a glass vase with her favorite flower the Challis

Lilly sitting on a night stand with a picture that had

inscribed on the base everlasting love, this stood out

because it was a relic of the past it was the given to the person a person that was supposed to be there with her forever but instead where it ended up was in a box that was sentenced to the dump. She rescued it and realized the best place was with her the giver of a gift that was so unappreciated. Oh what a difference a day makes. This was her new day to head in the direction that was unknown to her but one that was designed for her before she even came into existence. As she lay pondering the ambiance of her surrounding a new surrounding she designed and thinking of her picture with the everlasting inscription she knew wherever she goes the Keeper of her body, mind and spirit the Lord orders her steps and directs her path . This will be a glorious day.

As she had done since the day he was born, she crept into her son's room and stood watching him breathe in and out. She never seems to amaze her how she could have been given such a wonderful gift by God. This child was the most precious thing in her life and the love she had for him was eternal, she touched his head and he stirred, she thought 'don't wake up it is Saturday no school today , you sleep her baby she was going to make you the breakfast of your dreams.

Cassi went to her room proceeded into the bathroom and started cleaning up she brushed her teeth after which she got undressed went into the bath and started the shower. As she stood letting the water roll over her shoulders she had a flash back to a screen of happier times standing just as she is now and suddenly feeling body warmth behind

her and them feeling strong arms enfolding her and then

ring!!! Ring! Oh the phone who could be calling at this

time of the morning well they are going to voice mail she

still have to finish this shower... she hurried and

complete the shower and toweled off and went into her

room put some clothes on and picked up the phone and

checked the number on the call display, oh its Mom. Her

mom was her rock she called her since this separation

almost every other day. She knew her Mom was a

worrier and right now the object of her worry was she

and her son until thing became stable in her mind she

would be on the lookout 24/7. This did not bother her in

the least her Mom was he best friend she never judged

her only supported and stood by her through thick or thin. In fact all members of her family was great they were a close family each one looking out for the other one. Umm... she said she will give Mom a call later today is Saturday lost of stuff to do to get settled in.

Cassi mind drifted again and wondered if her husband< Oh he's the former husband now is even thinking of her. Unlikely but she knew for a long time she will always think of him she had loved that man. Even through the hurt and pain, she had given her heart to him and although he sought to return it after , stepping on it spitting on it , she still could not shake the or forget the very few times of good, tenderness or forget the smile that said what she thought it said she care and she love you... She remembered times when she would just look at this man whom some would not consider to be handsome anyway and see the most beautiful looking creature in the form of a man standing before here. They say love is blind but deaf and dumb is following suit rapidly and frankly there is a tug of war for which one to be on top...

Cassi knew it would take tons of work on her person more than counseling to get over that man; in fact another man must capture her heart more profoundly than he did to set her free from the obsession of the loss of a love that never was...

One would think a woman who so many men declared as beautiful, intelligent and the whole package was so self assured that the emotional turmoil she was going through

of which no one knew because she was a master at hiding

the hurt even though she would talk, cry about what

happened... But the through feeling never surfaced for

anyone to see. She would by this time gotten pass it.

But in truth once you really love someone you can never

unloved them unless you desire to do so. Though you

may dislike what they have become or what they do you

never hate them. Love is a choice not a feeling.

Journey continues...

Confront the dark parts of yourself, and work to banish them with illumination and forgiveness. Your willingness to wrestle with your demons will cause your angels to sing. Use the pain as fuel, as a reminder of your strength."- August Wilson quotes <u>(American Writer, 1945-2005)</u>

NOTHING TO FEAR BUT FEAR IT SELF'

Cassi never believed that she would ever be at a point in her life where uncertainty, apprehension and mistrust and in some case self doubt would plague her life.

During her time in counseling one of the hardest t aspects so self f evaluation she had to deal with was insecurity. Doubt had become such a close companion of her life handling her family finances in making decisions especially in her personal relationships. For every decision she made she set about diagnosing it life she was in a court room, acted as Lawyer, Jury and Judge, she was determine to reach the best decision in any matter. The prospect of making the mistakes and bad decisions of the past was no longer an option.

So what can she do now about this constant insecurity further discussion in therapy was not an option both financially or by desire all had been said that was needed to be said? She knew she had to find a way to deal with her fears and put them to rest.

While watching a TV show one evening about people who faced their fears of such things like heights, insects and so forth, Cassi thought what was her physical fear and she knew immediately it was being up high. Even though she had traveled extensively via airplanes, she had worked and been in many high rise buildings and even rode some of the most terrifying roller coasters at Six Flags Cassi always felt some inward fear. In a high rise building she never ever got close

to window and looked down. She always kept her eyes

closed while riding the roller coaster and she always sat in

the isle seat which on any air plans she even while riding in

the elevator shuffle to back and hang on to the hand rail until

it stopped and she was able to get off. Cassi was a master at

coping in challenging situations; adaptability was one of her

strong suits.

Cassi knew she had to face the woman in the mirror and she

had to ensure that person was no one else but her authentic

self.

Eureka!! She knew what she could do the thought just popped in her head like a lightening flash. She could face her fear by going to one of the world's tallest structure "The CN Tower". She would go and do the most daring thing possible and that is lie on the glass floor.

Cassi struck to her guns and the following Saturday she took her son and they visited the CN Tower.

Just standing outside the Tower and looking up was scary, for a moment Cassi felt like there was no way she could go through with it, but her son who she lovingly called her "Fearless Fred" said then " Mom its going to be fun, plus she'll be there be there too and guess what less than half your age, so you should be encouraging me' not the other way around'. Cassi looked at him and burst out laughing, "Ok big man let go in'.

They bought their tickets n and looked around then they decided they would enjoy some of the attractions on the ground floor. There was a simulated ride which seems interesting that would get them warm up for the big event... Cassi and her son entered the ride and it started transporting them to a log manufacturing company. In the simulations they were logs going through processing. It was fast, furious and scary, they got wet, went up high trails and dropped into deep pits, when it ended Cassi son said "Lets do it again and they did. After the ride they took the elevators and when to the view point, 360 degree circular view. Normally elevators take seconds but this seems like 30 minutes.

At the top they decide to leave the view for the last, so they visited the stores and decided to get a bite. Again Cassi felt a tinge of fear, but looking at the eager expression on her sons face made her just feed off his enthusiasm.

Finally it was their turn walked around viewing the city of Toronto from 446.5meters up that is 1464.9 ft in the air. When they reached the glass floor before she could stop him Cassi son got unto the floor and started jumping on it like all the people around him. Cassi heart went to her throat she screamed for him to come off it., everyone looked at her surprised and some even said calm down Mom its 'OK " he won't fall…Cassi son stopped immediately and rushed to her seeing the terror in her face, he hugged her tightly and said " Mom its OK she am fine". Cassi hugged him like crazy then he let of off her and started walking slowly back once he was

on the glass floor again he reached out to her and said "

Mom come get me" without knowing it as if mesmerized,

she reached out and took his hand. He said let move over

here and they moved to the clearest spot on the glass floor,

then he said lets sit which they did. It was at this point Cassi

looked down and saw only dots on the floor nothing from

that vintage point were recognizable on the ground.

Surprising thing was Cassi did not feel any fear at that point

she felt like she was floating in air. Maybe it was the still

small voice of a child; 'her child' which calmed her fears or

something greater than what she could imagine that id it.

Then she did what she came to do and lye down on the glass

floor. From that point on Cassi knew for sure the only thing

to fear was fear itself.

But friendship is the breathing rose, with sweets in every fold. -Oliver Wendell Holmes

FRIEND

During the time of self analysis and revitalization and restoration, Cassi met Sean who reached out to me thorough a chat site for black people on line. She opted to put her profile online with the hopes of meeting and making new friends male and female all around the world. This was an attempt to broaden her horizons and who knows she might find potential friends i.e. male who could lead to something more.

Sean sent me a flirt message and although after reading his profile She thought he was interesting he mentioned he wanted for potential mates only casual relationships and although this was not her requirement for all the male contacts she made some if their profile sounded solid and strong and she saw them as a potential mate must want to have a long-term relationship or she would not correspond with them. But with Sean she let her reservations down and sought to discover more about him. Cassi and Sean chatted on line for a long time then she decided she wanted verbal communication so she gave him her number. ore and more Cassi and Sean chatted on –line fore a while more and during that course of conversations she found him to be as he fondly called himself smooth and slow like molasses.

Unlike the others who wanted to meet me right away because as they put it to her "you are sooooooo.... beautiful" and she as well as the world knew their imagination is running wild and they think another pretty girl to bed... But little did they know this girl is not another pretty but dumb chick she have integrity and smarts to boot... With Sean Cassi immediately knew she had found a new life long friendship, like no other. She recall their first conversation it was about spiritual matters chatting for over 2 and half hours to a man who was not in the church who had a belief in God but had not solidified a relationship with him and as they spoke it became a process of her witnessing to this man evangelizing about the God she served and how he had made all the difference in her life. He shared his battle with cancer and him surviving that ordeal and him living with the knowledge that although in remission it could reoccur, how this impacted his life. The discussion became so energizing and uplifting at its conclusion that she did not want to end it if it weren't for the fact we were both exhausted and had to work that day to attend she could continue chatting for hours.

After that day hardly a day passed when she did not chat with Sean apart when he was out of country. She had to make him leave his laptop and blackberry at home to not be in touch with her or anyone while he was vacationing...

Now the irony about their relationship was that underneath the very platonic relationship they had there was a level of guardedness because they both agreed there was a physical attraction and yes at times they flirted but never crossed that line either verbally or physically. They could watch a movie and snuggle up on the couch together like old lovers and other times be just like a sister and brother, but never have they even tried or attempted to elevate the relationship into anything intimate. They knew they had a good thing going a genuine friendship some thing men and woman struggle to do as adults without becoming romantically involved.

How could she describe her friend? He was manly , very good-looking, sexy as hell ... yes she said it because it was the truth he was a sexy dude, smart as well , financially secure and emotionally open as well, caring honest and trustworthy...A good father to his kids and a good friend caring neighbor and diligent worker.

One hears her speak about this man and you think she was his complete cheering squad in some ways she was the head cheer leader but he is what is he, and what she appreciate as a friend not fake and absolutely honest, and she was only say this because he always call her "beautiful" as a nick name but because it is true.

For a while and even now she still reassess the friendship and revaluate, wondering if it will stand the test of time , of spouses, of challenges and diversities cause she knew how they will come one day. Cassi sees him at times in this manner as how "life the epitome of the man" she would like to spend the rest of her life with and other times like the coolest brother a girl could have.

Sean and her have grown close and will she was sure grow closer he has shared many a things with me even his many escapades with the many ladies in his life and his romantic intent with regards to them . She was sure if these women knew they would drop him as a bad habit but they will...

They have spoken openly about their interest with regard to

finding that one true love in each of our lives our future

plans and such like. By invitation Cassi met his family

which he made a point of stating how much of a big deal that

was...he met hers not by design but even so he did some of

hers. There was and in some cases she thought how great it

would be to have her best male friend as her life partner, but

she know they would never be more it would spoil the

quality and substance of what they have the song Nobody is

Suppose to be here `by Debra Cox runs through her mind all

the time when she thought of him. But the pleasure of a

season is not worth the lasting life long relationship. Sean is

and will always be that line of a song `wonderful you are to me 'he made an impression on her and continues even now

not only as a friend but had life been different the man who

would be put the `AH `in her sigh...

As your faith is strengthened you will find that there is no longer the need to have a sense of control, that things will flow as they will, and that you will flow with them, to your great delight and benefit.

Emmanuel Teney

ON MY OWN

Cassi realized that now she needs to structure her life with new hopes and aspirations. Dating had become a frustrating process most of the men she met where not ready to commit to an honest, equitable, caring relationship.

She put new energy into letting go of her doing the work if searching for Mr. Right. She decided that if it is in Gods will whoever that life partner is will be united with her in time. This lent a tremendous relief to her as "lets face it "she was not getting any younger but she was absolutely wiser than she ever was the saying with aging comes experience and wisdom was definitely true.

Cassi was always a lover of knowledge and reading gave her the opportunity to build that knowledge base. During this time she sought to be more introspective. She felt she still had more work to do to overcome the failed decisions of the past and to a new mind set to enable her to make better decisions.

She decided to finally use her library card; she started reading a lot of books about self improvement and the understanding of human behavior. For Cassi she now wondered how to apply all this knowledge to her own life, she remembered a passage of the bible Psalm 51: 10-12 which states:

Create in me a clean heart, O God,
and renew a steadfast spirit within me.

Do not cast me away from your presence
and do not take Your Holy Spirit from me.

Restore to me the joy of your salvation
and sustain me with a willing spirit.

Cassi realized all that happen was in the past; even though she will never forget she knew she had to for give not only those whom she thought did her wrong but she had to forgive her self to re-knew her spirit her inner man to be made whole.   There is a statement that a man and in this case a woman is not measured by what they have but by the extent of their character and to build the right character your inner being must be at peace and joy that surpasses all understanding can be yours.

Being on her own without marriage , a partner and facing all

the challenges of single parenthood, building a life solely

on her strength of self which is her own abilities, knowledge

, and endurance can now be done without worry or stress .

Because now she had a great inner peace and more assured

than ever that she was not the one in control; God was and he

is the one who will guide and direct her path as he has

always done. The path might be challenging at times but in

but he remind us in the in His word through the Holy Bible

Hebrews 13- 5 and Deut 31-6 that' he will never leave us or

forsake us'.

In every conceivable manner the family is the link to our past and the

bridge to our future (Alex Haley)

THE FAMILY TIES THAT BIND US TOGEHER

The saying blood is thicker than water is always used when

referring to family ties. Dedication, Loyalty, Respect and Love.

With all choices that life offers us naturally one thing is

predetermine for us a birth and that is what family we are born

into. And good or bad or development and growth uncannily are

not determined by which family we are born into.

Cassi had a large family so extensive it was hard for her to keep

track of them all and maintain the family ties. After growing up in

a large extended family Cassi knew that one important aspect of

her success in relationships was learning how to maintain her

family ties.

Her parents were hard working people who sought to give and her and her siblings a life far better than they ever had.

Her mother was a selfless, kind hearted and deeply spiritual woman whom raised not only her 5 children but 6 adopted children whose biological parents were either dead or too poor to provide for them with the necessities of life. She was a professional care giver a nurse it was a natural for her as breathing to seek to look after the less fortunate. Cassie mom always used the term" David said I was young yet now I am old but I have never seen the righteous forsaken nor their seed begging bread" taken from the Psalms. This was a prophetic statement to which Cassie always applied to her life when ever she had to face a challenge or obstacle. Cassie mom believed steadfastly that the good or bad you do in your lifetime will be passed on to you or your offspring and every generation to follow; one could call it "karma".

Many lives have been touched by her mother's willingness to give of her love and support to care of others expecting nothing in return. Cassie while she grew up realized those traits from her mother of giving, caring, sharing and loving was a part of her. , Sometimes she thought it was so difficult to say 'No", it had gotten her into real trouble from time to time yet she felt it was better to give than to receive.

Cassie father was a man you could call an 'Alpha male'. He was in charge of his life and that of his family. A protector, provider he ensured everything and everyone pertaining to him was taken care of in everyway. From a young age he had learned to take care of himself, not from the traditional nuclear family structure he was passed off to uncle to be raised. He was never regarded as a sibling but more so a servant , nonetheless he accepted his statue in life and rose above his challenging circumstances and absorbed life like a sponge he excelled at everything he did academics, trade and work. He was a stanch believer in lifelong learning he instilled that principle into his children. He was a strong disciplinarian especially with his kids however he was not legalistic in nature but did ensure his families adhere to a set of rules he prescribed to. Cassie loved and respected her father, the life lessons he taught were to have perseverance to overcome challenges of property and everything associated with it, as well as learning how to implement love and care in your life so that you can be a successful human being.

In the list of her siblings Cassie was somewhere in the middle. You know the place that is sometimes overlooked, you're old enough and smart enough to understand the grievances of the oldest child and you are cool enough to "hang" with the youngest child.

Cassi found the role also lent to her being mediator of both young and old. Yet even though many challenging issues from time to time between her brothers and sisters, she was able to be the voice of reason... Cassi mused over this ability and thought, if you related her brother and sisters to social animals or in this case mammals in a hierarchy community her brothers would be 'Alpha' and her sisters would be 'Omega'.

Cassi siblings were devoted, loyal, respectful and loving of each other. They always had the other persons back regardless of circumstances. This human character trait her parents had instilled that family always comes second right after God being first in your life.

This quote by 'Thich Nhat Hanh a Vietnamese Monk said it best -"If you look deeply into the palm of your hand you will see your parents and all the generations of your ancestors, all of them are alive in this moment, each is present in your body. You are the continuation of each of these people your family."

Overtime these life lessons served Cassi well. After every obstacle and challenge she faced in life she knew she had the support of her family, because there was always ties that bind them together of love, loyalty.

'Depart from Evil, Seek Peace and Pursue it." Psalm 34:14

PEACE

The etymology **Peace** ....a word having such various meaning such as :- *dovish, peace-loving, mild, non-violent, non-belligerent, unbelligerent, unwarlike, non-warring, non-combative, temperate, agreeable, compatible, congenial, , friendly, amicable , cordial, serenity, calm, quiet, harmony.*

Cassie loved reading about different cultures and what was an inspiring culture to her was that of the biblical Hebrews. The term 'Shalom" which is a peace greeting also held the most relevant meaning for the word Peace because it spoke to wholeness as seen in Genesis 43: 27, but still Cassie also desired what can be referred to as an inner peace.

It is stated a healthy homeostasis, inner peace is having a state of being equipped "mentally and spiritually. Cassie journey of self discovery took her to many challenging areas which at the end of the day she hoped that would acuminate into a peaceful end.

In 1651 Thomas Hobbs used the Term " *nosce te ipsim*" which translated means " read thyself", in short what it is saying is studying the emotions, character and attitudes of people through books is good but people are walking books just living and experiencing people on a interpersonal basis is best way in knowing them and yourself.

Cassi faith taught about peace. The bible teaches to appreciate the meaning of peace it should be understood as it relates with grace.

Every monotheistic religion teaches of Peace. The word Islam means 'peace' as it comes from the word "Astama "which means to surrender oneself. The Hebrew "Shalom" is the underlying principle of the holy book thee Torah. In Christianity the bible teaches "Jesus is the Prince of Peace, so wanting to have inner peace appears to be what most faith recommends as a good principle in life.

Goodwill, respect and justice have been principles of which Cassi has lived by. In her life Cassi had turmoil especially interpersonal relationships and as she tried to understand and resolve those challenges. Many had referred to her as a Pacifist, always exercising non-violence and looking to find a harmonious and unified solution to any conflict.

Peace what a profound term. Cassie pondered it even more, with a smirk on her face she thought "every beauty queen favorite statement is "I want world peace', this is in answer to the question what would you like to happen, however for Cassie it was more like hoping to be first place in a race but then 'alas' you just realize you have no feet your in a wheel chair.

Untitled prayer by theologian Reginald Niebuhr

Serenity Prayer

God grant me the serenity to accept the things I can't change

Courage to change the things I can

Wisdom to know the difference

"AH"

Cassi was a woman who made her faith her life. In good

time and in bad the Bible had been her source of

encouragement and no other scripture captured the essence

of how she reverenced god Like this psalm, it was to her as

Oprah had said her " Ah moment ".

The LORD Is My Light and My Salvation
A Psalm of David.

The LORD is her light and her salvation;

Whom shall she fear?
The LORD is the strength of her life;
Of whom shall she be afraid?
When the wicked, even mine enemies and her foes,

came upon me to eat up her flesh,
They stumbled and fell.
Though a host should encamp against me,

her heart shall not fear.

though war should rise against me,
In this will she be confident.
One thing have she desired of the LORD,

that will she seek after;
that she may dwell in the house of the LORD
all the days of her life,
to behold the beauty of the LORD,
And to inquire in his temple.
For in the time of trouble he shall hide me in his pavilion:

in the secret of his tabernacle shall he hide me;
He shall set me up upon a rock.
And now shall mine head be lifted up

above mine enemies round about me:
therefore will she offer in his tabernacle sacrifices of joy;
She will sing, yea, she will sing praises unto the LORD.
Hear, O LORD, when she cry with her voice:

Have mercy also upon me, and answer me.
When thou sadist, Seek ye her face;

her heart said unto thee,
Thy face, LORD, will she seek.
Hide not thy face far from me;

put not thy servant away in anger:
thou hast been her help;
leave me not, neither forsake me,
O God of her salvation.

When her father and her mother forsake me,

Then the LORD will take me up.
Teach me thy way, O LORD,

and lead me in a plain path,
Because of mine enemies.
Deliver me not over unto the will of mine enemies:

for false witnesses are risen up against me,
And such as breathe out cruelty.
she had fainted, unless she had believed

To see the goodness of the LORD in the land of the living.
Wait on the LORD:

be of good courage, and he shall strengthen thine heart:
Wait, she says, on the LORD.

Published by The American Bible Society

"Our lives begin to end
The day we become silent about things that matter."-
Rev. Martin Luther King, Jr. Civil Rights Leader

What Keeps Her Going...?

Cassi had asked herself the that question time and time

again and after every occasion of joy , every sensation of

'exhalent' every period of pain and grief through it all, "what

keeps her going'?

Who was she? Well she was average by her examination of

her physical appearance even though in the eyes of some

especially men ('many of whom will lie to Jesus' to get a

foot in the door of heaven'), have said to her - you are

beautiful, pretty, cute all the catchy words that they hope will get me to be in a horizontal position so that they may hear

her say it is all yours, have a field day with this body.

"Ah'... But alas she was not one of the plenty of fishes in the

sea that gets hooked on any and every bait being thrown out

there, regardless of how that bait is seasoned. She was not

the girl who walks with the chip on her shoulder or the belief

that she got it going on so she must 'show it off". Cassi was

just happy that God put every thing in the right place the

eyes, nose and mouth are where they should be and the

hands and feet keep her mobile and above all as her mother

always says" she wake up every day in her right mind"..

Cassi was well aware in a moment in a twinkling of an eye

any thing can change especially since she know age is no

respecter of persons we will grow old and looks will change. Beauty fades so her looks do not keep her going...

Spirituality is a foundation of her existence she had a profound belief in God and she lived by her convictions and beliefs. Her steps in life are ordered by the God, he directs path, and this is her conviction. Even though they may not always materialize the way she hoped, there is always a purpose for everything that happens in her life. Life is not a random act or circumstance and inasmuch as we are not operating as pawns in the universe under the watchful eyes of an Almighty God he has enabled us with the innate ability of choice. So Spirituality is vital to what keeps her going.

Wisdom coupled with intelligence is desired it is achievable it is good, but will that keep you going? As for being smart she can say that she can accredit herself as being quiet better than most this is not ego for her to say because it is a fact. She had uncommon intelligence that academic degrees have not lent their name too. Wisdom is a God given gift and that has been given to her. But does that drive her? Certainly, she seeks to use whatever knowledge she had to enhance her life and that of the people around her.

Now as a black woman who is a single mother and parent yes that sole statement does play a factor in what drives her and keeps her going. As a black woman working in Canada she had everyday strived to be not only on par but better in work ethic and efficiency than that of her pairs. . Most black women especially immigrants like her have ventured into the atypical careers; teachers, nurses a lawyer or two and majority working in major manufacturing companies, but for her working in corporate industries in middle management or senior management position have been a rarity amongst her pairs in Canada . For Cassi she has been blessed that the opportunities she had and so she worked arduously to ensure that none of it have goes to waste

As a mother raising a child who is a black male in this society she was faced with a whole other set of situations. The society say 50% of young black men are in prisons or pursuing criminal activity, many under educated, and many die before their 30th birthday. Many would argue she had the decked stacked against her and it is stacked against her son by him being black. But we as a family unit do not operate in the skepticism or society predetermination of our chances of survival; we chart our course with the help of God by our skills and abilities. She believed that they can do anything they needed to survive and she had instilled that attitude in her son. She had adhered to that mindset for her own self progression. There have been times of trials times of grief times of joy and happiness. Yet being a mother she would never trade for anything else in the world. She marvel and worry at the same time about her child's future and theirs together but she know she would never feel whole without having been a mother. Motherhood and Parenting YES it keeps her going.

Daily living, what is that? Working and paying bills. Does that keep you going? It will, whether we want it to or not. In today's modern world it is what we do. However we derive an income legally or not work is done to achieve it and then that income is used to acquire what we need to survive, food, shelter and clothing. Lets face it there are no freedom roads and she believes if there was one, we most certainly pay travel on it.

As for work, getting the pat on the back or hearing the words " well done" is so rare it is expected that you 'perform your job as required and job satisfaction is overrated because of this lack of appreciation. To most as is to her it is a mean to an end. So at this point lets check the scale factor does that keep her going it does because it has to, Because if it does not " she could be wearing a card board sign in the streets of downtown Toronto standing over a steamed manhole which states " help her or spare change please. "So work has to keep going on.

Social and Community life can be a driving force in many peoples life. She found great satisfaction in community service. Yes she can be classed as a giver in every facet of her life. We are all called to give back and she had never wavered from the belief that whatever you give out will come back to you whether it is good or bad.

So what is left Love? Relationships with family and friends is vital in personal development learning to maintain them is encouraging and fulfilling. Her family is a close group and they always protect, encourage and in some cases help to provide for each other. Her friends are few but like family they are supportive in many ways and life would never be same without them.

Lastly "Love of a Man" the most intimate relationship, that of a partner, spouse, husband.   We could use many sad songs to describe this aspect of our life. It kept us going, "Yes" in many directions some we would prefer not to have gone at all?   But we say this ""Gnothi Seauton"-Knowing oneself- Knowing yourself is not beliefs or ideas floating around in your mind it is your sense of who you are determines what you perceive as your needs and what matters in your life and what matters should be truth. The real love of a man to a woman can be a driving force that makes one aspire to be more to be the compliment of each other. Every woman or man seeks this and we are no different. We should look at the question "what keeps us going " We should look at all the parts that make up the whole of us, ... For her a young single black woman these are the priorities- God , her child , work, daily living , community service relationships of family and friends and the love of a deeply spiritual and wholesome man. These are all a part of the circle of life so in one way or the other does keep her going, "

ACKNOWLEDGEMENT

I CAN`T BEGIN TO ACKNOWLEDGE ALL THE PEOPLE – who

has influenced, inspired or encouraged me in putting together

this project. I am a lover of knowledge, a lover of truth, a

lover of people, a lover of books and I love God.

So many books have inspired me to clarify my thoughts and

understanding. They have helped me in knowing myself

each day; however I will single out above all the most

important book in my life the Holy Bible of which many

quotes are given throughout this book. I have also included

quotes from many of the world most influential an notable

history makers stemming from Buddha a spiritual teacher to

civil rights leader Martin Luther King and other current day

notables such as my personal inspiration Miss Oprah

Winfrey.

Special thanks to **MY** family, starting with my son Tyrone

he is a brave, smart young man and the champion encourager

to all my hopes and aspirations , one day he will be known as

a wise man who truly knows himself, he is truly brilliant

beyond his 12 years. I credit my parents Gladys and Caswell

Brown for their encouragement and support but special

mention of my Dad who started me on my pursuit of

knowledge, by forcing me to read the local news-paper every

page front to back ensuring in the process that not one word

was missed or miss-pronounced at the tender age of 10 years

old. Special thanks to my brother Raymond and my Sis

Oona for their support as well. Special mentioned of my

friend Lisa, whom was gracious in lending me her computer

to finish my editing of this project, Girl!! Once the first

revenue comes in, we will go sit on a Patio and have our

beloved "Virgin Pina Colada"

The idea for this book came through various life experiences

but also from reading a book that changed my life it is

**The Power of Now** ,by _Eckhart Tolle._

Again, I thank all supporters and everyone. **_BLESS_**

About the Author

Mervis Brown is a single mother, daughter, sister, niece, aunt, grandchild, grandaunt, cousin and friend. After migrating for a better life from her native Jamaica she worked studiously to not only improve and enhance her life but to do the same to all whom she encountered. Her love of books started in High School where she made it her mission to read on a per book basis everything available in print for an author. She continued in her passion of reading but later found it liberating sharing her own vibrant imaginative mind through writing.

This book is a work of fiction with ideas based from life experiences it has enabled this author to shine a light on the many popular and common beliefs that evade our

society. Along with writing books Mervis also a sketch

artist and is currently employed fulltime in the financial

services field and in addition pursues another of her goal a

law degree.

www.ingramcontent.com/pod-product-compliance
Lightning Source LLC
Chambersburg PA
CBHW030337020726
47493CB00004B/1310